On the edge

Sleeping with the Fishes

Mike Gould

Folens

© 2003 Folens Limited, on behalf of the author.

United Kingdom: Folens Publishers, Apex Business Centre, Boscombe Road, Dunstable, LU5 4RL.
Email: folens@folens.com

Ireland: Folens Publishers, Greenhills Road, Tallaght, Dublin 24.
Email: info@folens.ie

Poland: JUKA, ul. Renesansowa 38, Warsaw 01-905.

Editor: Kay Macmullan
Layout artist: Suzanne Ward
Cover design: Duncan McTeer

First published 2003 by Folens Limited.
British Library Cataloguing in Publication Data. A catalogue record for this publication is available from the British Library.

ISBN 1 84303 400–X

Contents

1 Meeting at the marina   5

2 Row, row, row your boat   12

3 Watery grave   22

4 The girl from the sea   30

5 Abandoned   32

6 Night visit   36

7 Problems and answers   40

8 Homecoming   45

The story so far

If you haven't read an *On the edge* book before:
The stories take place in and around a row of shops and
buildings called Pier Parade in Brightsea, right next to the
sea. There's Big Fry, the fish and chip shop; Drop Zone, the
drop-in centre for local teenagers; Macmillan's, the sweet
and souvenir shop; Anglers' Haven, the fishing tackle
shop; the Surf 'n' Skate shop and, of course, the Brightsea
Beach Bar.

If you have read an *On the edge* book you may have met
some of these people before.

Phil Johnson:	*his mum runs the fish and chip shop with Phil's step-dad, Ken.*
Mick King:	*lives with his mum, Sandra, and is keen to impress his dad, Frankie.*
Frankie King:	*Sandra's husband; owns a flat at the marina and nightclubs in the town.*

So, what's been going on?
Mick and Phil have a habit of exploring places where they
shouldn't be. The truth is, it's usually Mick's idea, but
somehow Phil finds himself unable to say no.

What happens in this story?
Mick and Phil steal an old dinghy down at Brightsea
Marina, but while larking about they hit an expensive
yacht. They don't like the look of the guy on deck – and
later realise just how evil he really is when they are forced
to help out in an emergency.

1

Meeting at the marina

Mick's dad, Frankie, lived in a posh flat down at the new marina.

To tell the truth, it was Mick's mum's flat as well, but she preferred to stay in their old terraced house in town.

His parents hadn't exactly split up, but Mick's dad wasn't around much at home. On the surface, Mick's mum didn't seem to mind.

"That's just your dad," she'd say.

Sometimes, Mick would go down there and look up at the top floor – the 'penthouse suite' as his dad called it. If he was lucky, his dad would let him in, but usually when he buzzed on the intercom, his dad said he was occupied, 'doing business'.

Mick reckoned it was something dodgy.
Often, he had seen gleaming sports cars
pull up outside, and men in suits shaking
his dad's hand.
Sometimes things were taken out of the
boots of the cars and carried in.
Mick had asked his dad once who all the
visitors were, but all his dad would say
was, "Never you mind, son, never
you mind."
Part of Mick admired his dad, always
looking sharp, always making a deal.
Part of him – the part he never showed
– thought his dad could spend a bit more
time with him, rather than wining and
dining his business friends.

It was a cool summer's evening.
School had finished and Mick and his
best mate, Phil, were hanging around
the marina.
There wasn't much else to do.
At least when school was on you had a
place where you could see your mates.
Now, half of them were working in the
town centre, half were off on holiday.

The clubs, restaurants and bars of the marina were out of bounds as they were too expensive.

But Mick and Phil liked hanging around the yachts in the quieter areas of the marina.

People-watching.

There was always someone to make fun of from a distance.

"Look at that."

Mick pointed at a sleek, white yacht – about 25 metres long – moored to the wooden decking on the other side of the water from where they stood.

At the stern sat a large, tanned man, sipping a glass of white wine.

A younger woman, possibly his daughter, emerged from below deck, carrying a plate of food.

He gestured roughly at her to put the food down, and then pointed at his glass.

She refilled it dutifully.

"Too good for you, Mick," said Phil.

"Wasn't her I was interested in," grinned Mick. "It was the food."

"Why don't you come back to the shop? Mum'll let us have some chips."

"No," replied Mick. "Can't be bothered. If my dad was in, he'd have something for us. He's got all sorts in that flat."

"Your dad's never in," said Phil, then immediately regretted it.

"What did you say?"

Mick turned away from the yacht.
He looked angry.

"Nothing," said Phil.

"At least my dad still lives here. Not like yours," Mick said savagely.

Phil was crushed.

For a while neither of them spoke.

It started to get dark.
Slowly, the flats around the marina lit up,
and people began to return to their boats
from their visits to the city centre.
Mick and Phil knew that, strictly
speaking, they shouldn't be in this part of
the marina.
You needed a special key, or a pass, but
Mick had figured out how to get in.
Besides which, he could always say, quite
truthfully, that his dad lived there.

Several people gave them funny glances
as they passed, but Mick just glared back
at them.

Eventually Phil spoke.

"Look, I'd better get back."

"Bit too dark for you, is it?"
mocked Mick.

"No, it's just … well, there isn't any point hanging round here all night."

Mick thought for a moment, then came over and punched Phil on the shoulder. It was meant to be playful, but it hurt.

"You're right, Phil. You're absolutely right. We can't let this rich lot have all the fun."

He set off down one of the walkways. He was almost running.

"Where are you going?" called Phil. "Wait up!"

He stood up to follow him, but by then Mick had already disappeared down another walkway, and Phil lost sight of him.
He would have gone after him, but he had the bikes to look after.
Trust Mick.

Phil sat down on one of the stone globes
used for tying up the boats.
Mick would be back when he was bored.

Half an hour passed; no sign of Mick.
Most of the boats were quiet now, except
for the odd person doing a spot of last-
minute repairs, or cleaning of decks.

Phil was seriously thinking of going.
It would serve Mick right if someone
nicked his bike.
Though whether anyone would want
Mick's rusty, mud-spattered old wreck
was another matter.

Just as he stood up to leave, he saw it.

At first he couldn't believe his eyes.
It was quite dark after all.
But, no … his eyes weren't
deceiving him.
It was Mick!
It was Mick, in a small wooden dinghy.
Rowing unsteadily between the two lines
of expensive yachts!

2

Row, row, row your boat

Mick stood up in the dinghy.
"What're you waiting for?"
Phil didn't move.
The water around the little boat looked
very black and very deep.
Also, it was now 9.30 pm – and Phil knew
his mum and step-dad, Ken, would
be worried.

Even though he was fifteen, Phil was
small for his age – and his parents tended
to think of him as younger than he
really was.
It annoyed him, but sometimes he didn't
want to grow up.
Mick seemed so much older, it felt
impossible he could ever be like him.

"Come on. It's only a bit of fun."
Mick sat down, and pushed the oars
into position.
Phil still hesitated.
"Five minutes – I promise. Then we'll
head back."
Mick smiled innocently.
"A little trip along this bit of water, then
back again. Go on – you know you
want to."
He could be quite charming when he
wanted to, thought Phil.

"All right – five minutes," said Phil,
finally, with a sigh.
He lowered himself carefully on to
the small floor of the boat, wobbled
unsteadily for a moment, and then sank
down on to the cross-seat opposite Mick.
Mick pushed the dinghy away from the
jetty with one oar, and the boat
drifted out.
He began to pull on the oars, rather
clumsily at first, then more powerfully,
pulling the boat towards the line of yachts
on the far side of the marina.

"Where did you get it from?" Phil asked.

"Poor little thing was squashed between two great big motor boats. It needed rescuing."

"You stole it, you mean."

"Borrowed. Anyway, who's gonna miss a little old boat like this?"

"The owner?"

"Yeah. When he comes back from one of those expensive bars. And that won't be till much later."

Mick looked over his shoulder.
"Stupid design, these rowing boats. Can't see where you're going."

"It's supposed to be like that," said Phil, shifting uneasily on his seat as the dinghy rocked about.

"You'll have to tell me where we're going, right?" said Mick.

Phil nodded, though to tell the truth, it was hard to see anything at all on the water itself.

The flats were lit up, of course, and in the distance, near the public end of the marina, he could just see the cafés and restaurants.

By now they had moved quite a way down the channel of water, but Phil couldn't be sure which direction they faced.

It was very confusing.

"Where are we, then?" Phil asked.

"Search me," Mick replied. "Somewhere near my dad's place, I think. Those flats might be near his. They all look the same."

Suddenly, Phil saw the stern of the large yacht they had been looking at earlier loom up out of the darkness.

It was still moored in the same place, so they couldn't have gone far.

However, down on the water in the little boat, the yacht seemed incredibly large, like a sleeping white shark.

Phil realised they were heading straight
for it.
"Watch it, Mick! Swing to the left, quick!"

Mick yanked his left oar.
The stern of the dinghy swung slowly
round and looked as if it would miss
the yacht.
But it wasn't enough.
The rowing boat clipped the rear of the
yacht, and then scraped horribly along
its side.

Phil groaned.
"Now we're for it."

Looking up, he could see the rich owner
they had watched earlier in the evening.
He emerged from below deck.
Now he could see him close up, Phil
didn't like the look of him.
His muscles bulged beneath his white
shirt, and he had a fat cigar clasped in
his hand.
There was no sign of the girl.
He marched to the edge of the yacht and
looked out into the blackness.
Fortunately, there were no marina
lights nearby.

"Keep your head down!" whispered Mick. "And don't make a sound!"

"Stop whispering, then," said Phil, pressing himself as closely as he could to the floor of the dinghy.

Then the man spoke.
At first, Phil thought he'd spotted them.
"There's no one there. Relax."
He stayed for a moment on the deck, and then took a long draw on his cigar, before puffing the smoke out into the darkness. Then he turned abruptly, and disappeared from sight.

Mick and Phil stayed still in the dinghy for several minutes, letting it drift gently on the water.
Then, when he thought it was safe, Mick rowed away from the yacht, past three or four other even bigger boats until they were in the middle of the channel between the two wooden platforms.

Phil was the first to speak.
"That was a close one."

"Yeah. Wouldn't like to get on the wrong
side of Mr Muscles."
Even Mick looked a little relieved.

"What about his boat? We damaged it,"
said Phil.

"A bit of paint. That's all it needs. Bet he
can afford it anyway."

"Yes, but …"

Mick gripped the oars, and interrupted.
"But what? Do you want to go back and
tell Cigar Man you did it? 'Cause I don't."

Phil looked at his watch.
"No … it's just … well, we shouldn't
be here."

"I've just as much right as anyone,"
said Mick. "That's my dad's place over
there, remember? And if my dad's
allowed in, then so am I, I reckon. Doesn't
matter that he hasn't got a posh boat.
Anyway, that bloke seemed more worried
about someone seeing him, than about us.
Probably not even his own boat."

Mick drew the oars through the water,
and steered the dinghy in the direction of
the lights in the buildings.

It seemed incredible that no larger boats
or yachts had crossed their bows, but they
were in a quieter part of the marina.
And it was getting late.
Still, there was something almost creepy
about being surrounded by all these
boats, with the distant sounds of traffic
and people almost blotted out by the slap
and slide of the oars in the water.

Phil yawned.
Five minutes Mick had said!
Five minutes?
It had been at least half an hour,
maybe more.
They'd better get back.
Return the boat before it was missed.

"I'm getting cold," said Phil.

"What d'you mean? It's summer."

"Yeah. That's why I'm shivering."

Mick stopped rowing.
"Always complaining, you are. I bring
you on a nice little trip, I even do the
rowing … and what do I get? Not a word
of thanks."

"It's been a laugh," replied Phil,
unconvincingly, "but we should
head back."

"All right, all right. You've made your
point. I'll head for the nearest jetty."

"What about the boat? The owner won't be able to find it."

"Give him something to do in the morning, won't it?" Mick laughed. "I can just see his face. 'I'm sure I left it here!'"

Mick began to pull again on the oars, and the boat edged slowly towards the nearest jetty, but it took a good four or five minutes before they were even close.

Then, having seen hardly anyone all evening, a familiar figure appeared by the side of the water.
It seemed incredible, but it was true.

It was the girl from the boat.

3

Watery grave

"Look," Phil said, pointing his finger towards the wooden jetty nearest to them. Sure enough, on the jetty could be seen the figure of a girl.

She was perhaps eighteen or nineteen years of age – it was difficult to tell. What was easier to tell was that she was drunk.

She tottered along the jetty, stopping occasionally to lean against one of the few upright lamplights.

She was wearing a pair of thin-looking jeans, and a flimsy t-shirt, and seemed to be shivering or shaking uncontrollably.

At first, they thought she was laughing. But then the truth hit them. She was crying. Crying in long, breathless sobs.

She took a couple more steps and reached the end of the jetty.
For a moment, she turned around and started to stumble away from the jetty edge.
But then her heel must have caught between the wooden slats, because she lurched forwards.
As she fell, she reached out with her hand and caught at a line running between the last yacht and the jetty edge.
But she missed it and, off balance, tumbled forward.

There was nothing to stop her fall.
She gave a half-cry, and then there was a loud splash.
One moment she was there.
Next she was gone.

For a moment the two boys were aware of the stillness of the black water all around them.
Time froze for a fraction of a second, then Mick sprang into life.
"She's fallen in, Phil!"

Phil felt his heart miss a beat.
Great – what a fantastic way to end
the evening.

Mick started rowing.
"Quick! You dive in, Phil! Grab her or
something. I'll bring the boat over. I can
row better than you."

Phil sat as still as stone.
"Phil! Get moving. She was drunk!
She'll drown!"

Phil looked at him with scared eyes.
"I can't, Mick."

"What? You've got to!"

"No. You don't understand."

"There's nothing to understand. Get in
the water!"

"No. It's not that. It's … I can't swim!"

Mick swore.

"Take the oars, then. Just my luck to be stuck with the only fifteen year old who lives by the sea and can't swim."

He stood up and pulled his sweatshirt off.

"Get the boat as near as you can to the jetty where she fell in."

With that, he balanced himself on the edge of the dinghy, then half-fell, half-dived into the water.

Phil could see him doing a clumsy front crawl, thrashing through the blackness towards the jetty.

Fortunately, it wasn't far.

Then, Phil lost sight of him.

He grabbed the oars and started to row.

It was difficult.

First, he had no one to guide him.

Second, his rowing wasn't great.

But he had to get the boat to the jetty.

It was a matter of life and death.

Somehow he managed it, listening out all the time for any sounds from the water.

Then he heard Mick's voice calling.
"Here, Phil! Over here!"
Phil swung the boat round as best as he
could, and tried to row towards the voice.

Suddenly, he was there.
He could see the girl's long, blonde hair
draped across her face.
But all he could see of Mick was his arm
under the girl's chin, holding her up.
Phil pulled the oars into the boat, and
leant over the side, trying to get his hands
under the girl's arms.
Despite her size, she was very heavy in
the water.
The jeans that had looked so lightweight
on her slim legs, now felt like lead pipes.

"I can't pull her up, Mick. She's
too heavy!"

"You've got to try, I can't hold on
much longer."
Mick was thrashing around, trying to
keep the girl's head up.

Then, out of the blue, the girl jerked into action.
The shock of the water, or Mick's actions must have pulled her out of her dream-like state.
Seeing the boat, she grabbed for the side.
Phil thought she'd tip it over.
But she didn't.
She held on to it tightly, and Mick, seizing his opportunity, let go of her head, and grabbed her waist below the water.
Then, with a superhuman effort, he lifted her.
Phil put his arms under hers and pulled, and Mick hoisted her legs over the side.
She flopped, like a wet sleeping bag, into the dinghy.

Mick, exhausted, clung to the boat, panting heavily.
The girl lay on her side, coughing and spluttering.

Phil managed to get the oars back into position, and rowed the last few metres to the jetty.
Mick hung on.

When he got to the jetty side, Phil flung
the dinghy's rope on to it, as far as
he could.
Then, cautiously, he pulled himself out.
Once on dry land, he grabbed the line and
tied it on to one of the mooring points in
a tight, if rather clumsy, knot.

Mick had managed to haul himself on to
the jetty.
He sat, dripping, on the wooden
platform, taking in long gulps of air.
"Got to … " he panted. "Got to … check
her. Check her breathing."
He dragged himself to his feet.

"No. She's OK. Look, she's sitting up,"
Phil reassured him.

Sure enough, the girl had raised herself
on to the seat, and was leaning forward,
her head in her hands.
Mick and Phil moved towards the boat
and put a foot each into it.

"Here," said Phil.

The girl looked up.

Her eyes looked frightened, like those of a small animal in the headlights of a car.

Then she swept her hair back from her eyes, and stood up.

Unsteadily, she climbed up on to the jetty.

She took one step forward, and then crumpled in a heap on the ground.

Mick and Phil hurried over, and turned her over.

Her eyes were closed, but she was moving her lips.

It was as if she was in a trance.

At first, they couldn't make out what she said.

Then, slowly it became clear.

She spoke with a strong accent but the words were unmistakable.

She kept on repeating them, as if she had learnt them off by heart.

"Hello. My name is Monica. I come from Kosovo."

4

The girl from the sea

Mick's sweatshirt was round the girl's shoulders, and she was now sitting up.

Looking at her closely, Phil could see how thin she really was.
If the two of them hadn't been there …
well, Phil didn't like to think about it.

Mick spoke.
"How much did you have then?"

The girl didn't understand.

Mick tried again.
"How … many … drinks?"
He mimed someone drinking from
a glass.

She shook her head, and spoke directly to them for the first time.
"No drink."

Mick looked at Phil.
"She's having a laugh. No drink? Who does she think she's kidding?"

Suddenly, the girl grabbed Mick's sleeve.
"No drink!" she repeated, fiercely.

Phil thought about it.
Perhaps it was true – the girl wasn't drunk now.
If she had had lots to drink, it wouldn't have left her system this quickly.

The girl got to her feet.
"Please." She looked at Mick and Phil.
"Take me to boat. Take me to man."

"All right," said Mick. "But when we get there, we leave you there, right? No need for us to meet The Man."
The girl nodded.

5

Abandoned

They eventually found the big yacht.
Or they would have done.
There was one slight problem.
It wasn't there.
Now there was a great big gap in the line
of boats.

The girl stood there, blinking, holding
back the tears.
"No boat."

"Are you sure this was the place?" asked
Phil, gently.

"Yes. I remember name of boat next to it.
Firefly."

Mick looked at the sleek, white and blue
yacht in front of them.
It had a fiery orange stripe down
one side.
"She's right. Look – there's the name."
Sure enough, there was 'Firefly', written
in long, curling letters.

Phil had been thinking about what
had happened.
About what the man had said.
"Relax. There's no one there."
Then, the girl appearing, as if drunk.
And what about the fact that the yacht
was no longer there?
He couldn't make sense of it.
"Surely he'll come back," Phil said.

The girl looked at him.
"No come back."

"How can you be sure?"

"He take my money. My passport.
Clothes. Everything."

"Why would he do that? If he's
your friend …"

Mick interrupted Phil, looking at him as if
he was an idiot.
"You don't get it, do you, Phil?"

"Get what?"

"Muscle Man wasn't her father, or
boyfriend. Or even a friend. She wanted
to get into England. Escape from Kosovo.
He was the last link."

The girl nodded.
"I give him money. All my money, and
my parents' money. He say, 'I get you
into England'. He say he get me passport.
Clothes. Job."

Phil began to understand.

"Then, when she got here," Mick added,
"Cigar Man must have drugged her. Put
something in her drink, then dumped her
on the jetty before sailing off."

"If we hadn't come along …" Phil began.

The girl looked up at him.
"Thank you," she said. "You save
my life."
She shivered.
Mick looked pretty cold too.

Phil spoke.
"We'd better report this. Get her to a
police station, then they can …"

But he didn't manage to finish
the sentence.
The girl's eyes opened wide, and, as
before, she spoke fiercely.
"No! Not police. They send me back!"

Mick and Phil looked at each other.
What were they going to do?

6

Night visit

Phil looked up at the tall block.
There were only a few lights on.
He guessed it must be close to 11 o'clock.
His mum would be doing her nut.

Mick had his hand pressed on the
rectangular metal button on the intercom,
next to the number 12.
The three of them were standing at
the foot of the block of flats, by the
front entrance.

"I knew it. He's not in. He never is."

He gave the buzzer one last push, waited,
and then sighed.
"Come on. No point waiting here."
He started to move away from
the entrance.

Then, a gruff voice spoke through the little speaker.
"Who is it?"

Mick turned, and ran up to the door.
"It's me, Dad. Mick."

"What do you want at this time of night? Does your mum know you're here?"

"Sort of. Look, can I come up? I need your help."

There was no answer, but after a few seconds there was a buzz, and Mick stepped forward.
"Come on."

The main door clicked open.
Mick pushed it and it swung back to reveal the lobby.
There was a large potted plant in the corner, and several modern paintings of ships on the walls.
It was all very classy.

Inside the lift, the mirrored glass showed
them how rough they all looked.
Mick and the girl were still dripping,
though their clothes had begun to dry
on them, and Phil looked dirty from the
efforts of the evening.

Mick's dad answered the door.
He was even shorter and stockier than
Phil remembered.
Phil had only met him a few times, even
though he'd known Mick for years.
He always expected someone taller, and
thinner, more like Mick.

He was wearing a white bathrobe, and
smelt of a strong aftershave.
He was clearly surprised to see the three
of them.
"I thought you was on your own. What's
goin' on?"

He looked at Phil and then at the girl.
Rather like a rattlesnake looks at mice.
"Who's she?"

"Look, Dad, I can explain everything. If we can just come in."

Mick seemed different with his dad.
Kind of afraid.
As if he was a little boy again.
Mick's dad didn't budge.

"We need your help, Dad."
Mick was almost pleading.

"This better be good, son," Mick's dad said, turning and walking back into the flat.

The three of them stepped through the door, and into Mick's dad's place.

7

Problems and answers

The girl was wearing a long bathrobe, one
belonging to Mick's mum.
She had had a hot shower and was now
curled up on the sofa, asleep.
The events of the evening had
exhausted her.

Mick and Phil had explained everything
to Mick's dad.

At the end of the tale, Mick's dad spoke.
"So, what's this got to do with me?"
He poured himself a drink from a bottle
in the drinks' cabinet near the kitchen,
and then stood looking out of the
window over the marina.

"You know what will happen if we turn her over to the police, Dad. They'll send her back."

"So what? It's not my problem."

Phil hadn't said anything since they'd arrived.
But he felt he had to help Mick out.
"She's a refugee from Kosovo. Her family's home was burned down. Her only chance is if she can send some money back. Help them get back on their feet."

"You could give her a job. In one of your nightclubs," Mick added.

Mick's dad turned to face them.
"You askin' me to break the law, son?"

Mick looked down at the floor.
Then, with an effort, he spoke.
"I've never asked you for a favour before, Dad. You always said I had to stand on my own two feet. But this is different. Please."

Mick's dad cast a glance at the girl, then back at them both.

"Where's she gonna live?"

"I … we … thought you might have some contacts."

"Did you now? Contacts, you reckon?" Mick's dad moved back towards the window.

He gestured towards another block in the marina.

"See that? A mate of mine's got a flat there. He's had to go away on a little holiday. Staying with Her Majesty for a while. I promised him I'd keep an eye on the place."

"So, she could stay there?"

"Only until he comes back. He could be back in three months. Depends. Could be longer."

Mick gestured towards the sleeping girl. "What about tonight?"

"Tell you what, son. As a special treat you can stay here too. But not a word to your mum about any of this. Our little secret."

Mick's dad walked towards the door. "By the way, son, remember, you owe me one."

It was clear to Phil it was time to leave. He cast one final glance at the sleeping girl, and then turned to go.
As he walked to the door with Mick, he spoke to him.
"I'm not sure that we're doing the right thing."

"So, what's your solution?" said Mick.

"Perhaps they wouldn't send her back. Especially if she's got a good case."

"What are you on about? 'Course they'd send her back!"

"They might not."

Phil lowered his voice.
"And what about your dad? Will she be all right working for him?"

"She won't get rich. He tells me he pays peanuts, but at least it's a job. I can keep an eye on her."

"She seems all right," said Phil.

"Yeah. She's all right. Nice."

Phil looked at Mick.
He was getting soft in his old age.
"Bit old for you, Mick, isn't she?"

For a moment it looked as if Mick was blushing.
Perhaps it was just the lighting in the flat.
"Don't be a prat. She's not my type."

Phil wondered what Mick's type was.
But he didn't comment.
"See you around," he said.

"Yeah. See you," said Mick, and shut the flat door.

8

Homecoming

It was 4 o'clock in the morning.
Phil sat in his room, his mum's words
still ringing in his ears from when he'd
arrived back home.

"Do you know what time it is? I've been
worried sick. Had to call Mick's mum
– she'd no idea where you were. And
coming back in that state. And losing
your bike. Fancy leaving it unchained
like that. And whatever possessed you
to borrow that dinghy? Well, you can go
back tomorrow and find it and apologise
to the owner. And you're grounded for
a month – no, make it two months. And
you're not seeing that Mick for a while
either!"

She had gone on and on.

His step-dad had said very little.
But he had asked him one question.
"So you weren't involved in that incident
with the coastguard at all?"

Phil didn't know what he was
talking about.

"Apparently, some chap in a yacht was
picked up out at sea. A friend of mine
works down at the boat yard. Told me
all about it. They found a whole load of
fake passports on this chap's yacht. And
drugs. He put up quite a fight. Nasty
bloke, he told me. Reckoned he'd been
involved with illegal smuggling,
or something."

Ken looked directly at him.
"But you didn't hear or see anything?"

Phil looked at his feet.
He didn't like to lie.

"They said this yacht of his had been moored at the marina. Funny thing was, someone had seen a girl with him. But she was nowhere to be found when they searched the boat."

Phil was about to confess everything.
But his mum came to the rescue, without meaning to.
She had noticed the oil stains on his sweatshirt.

"Look at him, Ken! He's only gone and ruined that new sweatshirt we bought him last week! Right. That's it, my lad. Off to your room. And you can clean that off yourself tomorrow. When you come back from the marina!"

Now he sat on his bed.
He hadn't slept a wink all night, even though he had felt absolutely shattered.

He stood up and went to the window.
Across the city he could see the lights from the marina.

Near one of those lights, the girl
was sleeping.
Or perhaps she was awake now.
In his own house he could hear
Ken snoring.
He wondered what her family was doing.
Were they sleeping?
Were they thinking about her?
Worrying about her?
Wondering where she was?
Whether she had somewhere to lay
her head?

He thought back to what had
happened earlier.

If they hadn't pulled her out of the water,
she'd have been sleeping all right.

Sleeping with the fishes.